Office Life (and Death)

by K C Murdarasi

Copyright 2015 K C Murdarasi

CreateSpace Edition

kcmurdarasi.com

Cover image (coffee stain) by Roger Karlsson, courtesy of
Free-Photo-Gallery.org

For Mr McDonald,
who gave two very soggy girls a lift into Glencoe.

Office Life (and Death)

Contents

Lies	7
The Business Trip	9
A Recipe for Summer	15
The Job Interview	21
Floor Six	25
The Head of Inequalities	33
Company Policy on Screaming	49

Office Life (and Death)

Lies

"The average person tells three lies a day," she read. She resolved to tell only two.

"Morning," said a colleague. "How are you?"

"Fine," she replied.

"Good weekend?"

"Not bad."

The rest of the day passed in silence.

Office Life (and Death)

The Business Trip

Anne was working late for the second time this week, and it was only Wednesday. She tried hard not to show her exasperation as her boss, Oscar Thornton, chatted casually into his Blackberry, obviously in no hurry to get on with the dictation. Anne was in a hurry. She was supposed to be going to the cinema with her sister. Oscar knew that, or he should if he ever listened to her. But he just carried on swapping terrible jokes with one of his equally annoying CEO pals.

Anne stood up to go back to her desk and get on with some work, but, barely looking at her, Oscar waved her back down. Now Anne was starting to get really annoyed. He could at least let her get on with something else while he kept her waiting. There were e-mails that needed replies – he never bothered to reply to his own e-mails. There were appointments that needed to be rearranged because, as usual, he had changed his plans at the last minute. And there were reams of annoying, unwieldy flipcharts that he wanted her to type up. All of this would still be waiting for her tomorrow if he kept her in his office listening to his blokeish phone conversation.

"Ha ha! No rest for the wicked!" said Oscar before finally finishing his call and turning to Anne.

"So, how far have you got?" he asked. Anne was incredulous.

"It's dictation, Mr Thornton," she reminded him, "I've been waiting for you." For the last twenty minutes, she felt like adding.

"Oh yes," said Oscar. "Forget it, I haven't got time to finish it now. You can just type up the flipcharts for the meeting. That'll do instead. E-mail them to me before 8.30am."

Anne tried to control her breathing. An hour late – the film would have started – and now he wasn't even going to bother? Her knuckles whitened around her dictation pad. She turned to go back to her own desk.

"And another thing, Anne," called Oscar, "why wasn't there any chocolate in your desk drawer today? I offered some to a client and it was embarrassing. Make sure it doesn't happen again."

That was the last straw. Anne knew that Oscar stole her chocolate, but to complain because there was none to steal! Letting out a shriek, she threw the dictation pad at her boss. She regretted it as soon as it left her fingers, but it was too late. The pad fluttered through the air like an angry white bird. Oscar started to turn, tried to duck out of the way, tripped. His flailing hand grabbed something to steady himself. It was the power cord for the hard drive. Oscar crashed to the floor and the drive slid off the desk and followed him. There was a thud, then silence. Anne tiptoed round the desk. Her hand flew up to her mouth. A hard drive can do a lot of damage to a human head. Hopelessly she checked for a pulse.

"I've killed him!" she squeaked.

Suddenly she heard a noise from the direction of reception. The cleaners! She looked around desperately for somewhere the hide the body. The shelved cabinet! Frantically she pulled out all of the removable shelves and stacked them at the bottom of the cabinet. Then she pushed the hard drive off Oscar's head, laid the dictation pad between him and the cabinet, and rolled him into place. It was hard to get it to close, but she was used to dealing with overstuffed cabinets and it took her only a few seconds. She popped the key into her pocket and listened. The cleaners must have gone through to the kitchen first, so she had another few minutes.

She surveyed the damage. There was blood all over the carpet, on the hard drive, and on her hands and cardigan. She darted back to her desk and grabbed the wet wipes out of her drawer, using up the whole packet in the space of a few minutes. She took off her cardigan and rolled it up around the used wipes and bloody dictation pad. Then she tried to lift the hard drive.

"Stop that!" came a voice from behind her. Trembling, Anne looked round.

"You shouldn't be lifting that on your own, love," continued the cleaner. "Let me help you." Together they lifted it back onto the desk.

"I hope it's not too badly damaged, or I'm in trouble!" said Anne.

"Don't you worry, I didn't see a thing," said the cleaner, winking. Anne smiled gratefully back at her, picked up her cardigan and went to get her coat.

"By the way," she said, as she walked out the door, "Somebody had a nosebleed in that room earlier. Maybe you could do something about the blood stain?" Then she left the office, stuffing her cardigan deep into the cleaners' black rubbish sack as she passed it.

Back in the office the next day, Anne waited to be discovered. She diligently started typing up Oscar's flipcharts to take her mind off the inevitable. At ten o'clock she remembered that Oscar was supposed to be giving a presentation in Edinburgh, so she called up and gave his apologies. Lunchtime arrived. Anne's friend Penny popped her head round the door.

"Coming?"

Anne couldn't face food. "No, sorry, there's something I've got to finish."

"Oscar's overworking you again," commented Penny, "Where is he today, anyway?"

"In Edinburgh. No, er, in London. He cancelled Edinburgh this morning."

"Typical Oscar!" said Penny, "I'm amazed you can keep up with his movements at all."

"Oh, you know, it's not that hard," said Anne, glancing towards the locked cabinet. The afternoon hours crawled by and eventually five o'clock came. Anne wiped up a small trickle of blood that had leaked from beneath the door of the cabinet, then went home.

The next morning, a Friday, Anne set about rearranging Oscar's meetings, postponing them by several weeks. She answered his e-mails, as usual, and checked his phone messages, as usual.

"Is he still in London?" asked Penny as they ate lunch together.

"Yes," said Anne, "he asked me to book him into the Hilton at the last minute."

"Typical Oscar!" said Penny. "It's lucky for him he's got such a good PA!"

Anne blushed.

In the afternoon she arranged disposal of the shelved cabinet for the Monday. The lock was broken, she explained, but the contents were unimportant and it could go to skip unopened.

Over the next few days and weeks Anne had many stabs of conscience and moments of fear, but she pushed them to the back of her mind and got on with her work. From her own computer she sent polite e-mails saying that Oscar would reply as soon as possible. From Oscar's Blackberry, which she held underneath the desk, she sent rude, badly spelled emails delegating every task to another member of the company. No-one noticed anything amiss.

"I haven't seen Oscar in ages," Penny said one day. "What on earth is he doing?"

"He's on a study trip to Australia," Anne said. "Somebody offered him free flights and accommodation while he was in London. Apparently they really lead the field down there."

"Alright for some!" tutted Penny, "I don't suppose we'll miss his useless arse much anyway."

Anne stopped sending e-mail replies from Oscar. She explained in her own polite e-mails that Mr Thornton had very limited access to the internet in Western Australia.

A few weeks after Oscar had taken his unplanned visit to Australia, he got a letter from the Board of Directors. They had heard about his trip and they demanded a full explanation, including a report on budgetary implications. Reading the letter, Anne realised that her charade had reached the end of the road. She filed the letter, as usual, then took a deep breath and set about writing a reply. That evening, Anne took a small amount of Oscar's personal items from his desk and disposed of them. The following evenings she did the same thing until there were none left.

A few days later the Board of Directors received a friendly but unrepentant letter from Oscar. He had just returned to the UK and received their letter. It was unfortunate that he had been unable to inform them of his trip beforehand, but "carpe diem" was his motto. The budgetary implications were non-existent in any case, thanks to the hospitality of his corporate hosts. Those hosts, whose identity he could not disclose under the circumstances, had in fact offered him a position here in the UK, and he had decided to take it. He thanked the Board for their understanding and wished them all the best in the future. The letter ended with Oscar's oversized, scrawly signature. As his PA, Anne had access to a scanned copy of his signature, of course.

Oscar rarely took a holiday, so he had enough annual leave days left to cover his notice period. He came in one evening to clear out his things – or at least, there was nothing left in his desk drawers afterwards – but no-one saw him. There was half-hearted talk around the office of a leaving party but Anne discouraged it. Oscar being Oscar, she said, he would probably decide at the last minute not to come, anyway.

Office Life (and Death)

The day after Oscar handed in his notice, Anne did the same thing. Penny was stunned but Anne explained that she felt like a change of direction. Besides, she had got used to Oscar and it would be strange to have to work so closely with someone new. They threw a leaving party for Anne, of course, who was well-liked. As she opened her presents and said goodbye to everyone over dinner in Topolino's, Anne almost regretted her decision – almost, but not quite. Her mind drifted back to the handover session she had given to the new PA that morning. The girl had asked her what Oscar had been like to work for. She had heard some horror stories from the rest of the staff.

"Oh, he wasn't as bad as all that," Anne said, "He could be quite nice sometimes. I can honestly say that for the last few weeks, Oscar Thornton was a dream to work for."

Glancing around, she leaned towards the girl's ear.

"And don't tell anyone," she whispered, "but he signed off a *very* generous leaving bonus for me just before he went."

A Recipe for Summer

Winner of Third Prize in Cwrtnewydd Scribblers Competition 2011
First published in *A Way with Words* anthology 2011

Rain. Buckets of it. Sheets of it. Dave looked out of the window and sighed.

"And this," he announced, "is supposed to be summer."

It was early June, but the sun had put in a meaningful appearance in the past couple of weeks less often than Dave had turned up early for work. He looked over to his colleague, Andy, who seemed not to have heard him. He was intently studying something that had arrived by post that morning. Dave walked round to Andy's desk to see it better.

"What's the book?"

Andy looked up.

"Mmm?"

"That book you're gawping at, what is it?"

"Oh, this." Andy's hand rested protectively over the book and for a moment it seemed that he would refuse to say. Then with a sheepish smile he admitted, "It's a book of aboriginal weather spells."

Dave guffawed.

"Spells? Here, give us a look."

He grabbed the book and flicked through. There were some words in mumbo jumbo and a lot of instructions relating to ingredients and method.

"Looks like a cookery book," he said dismissively, tossing it back.

Andy shrugged. "With this weather, I'm prepared to try anything."

Dave laughed again.

"Good luck to you, mate," he said.

At the end of the day Andy waited until Dave had gone home (on the crack of four fifty-five) before he took the book out of his drawer and slipped it into his bag. The weather had cleared up by the afternoon, but the forecast was for more rain the following day. Andy glanced doubtfully as his bag and shrugged.

The next day, as predicted, the rain continued. Not as predicted, however, it failed to clear up in the afternoon. Dave looked sulkily out of the window as he walked back from the kitchen, black coffee in hand.

"What is with this weather?" he moaned. "Does it never stop?"

Andy looked out of the window and said, "It does seem to be worse, doesn't it?"

"Your umbo bungo book doesn't work then," Dave commented sardonically.

"I suppose not," replied Andy neutrally, then went to make himself a weak tea, since Dave hadn't offered.

June wore on, but still the summer didn't come. In the first week of July the office was uncharacteristically empty since a number of people had taken as much as they could stand and had flown off to the sun for a week or two. Dave spent his time on the internet looking for cheap holidays, or moaning to the staff who remained. They gladly moaned back. Andy was the only one who didn't seem to be wilting in the constant rain.

"What's your secret?" a secretary asked him as she picked up her umbrella, ready for the trip home.

"My secret?" Andy echoed.

"How come this weather isn't getting you down? We've had no summer at all but I never hear you even mention it."

"Oh," said Andy, "um, positive thinking, I guess."

"Mm," said the secretary in agreement, not really listening, putting on her coat. Dave, who heard the conversation, noticed that Andy seemed to be blushing, which was strange – the secretary wasn't even nice-looking.

In mid-July Dave finally managed to find a cheap break to suit him, and headed off to Zante. He was relieved, when he got there, to find that the sun still existed. Disregarding all sensible advice, he offered his pasty body as a burnt sacrifice on the beach the first day, and spent the rest of the holiday wondering how it was possible for clothes to chafe so much. By the time he returned, his beetroot colour was peeling to reveal a warm beige tan. He was enjoying the comments from people who noticed his change of colour, and enjoying retelling the story of his epic sunburn, when his pleasure was dampened somewhat by realising that Andy also had a noticeable bronze tinge.

"Hi Andy," he said in a slightly cold tone, "I thought you said you were going to tough it out in the British summer. Where did you go?"

"What?" asked Andy, apparently nonplussed.

"The tan – where did you get it?"

Andy looked at the brown back of his hand as if noticing for the first time.

"Oh," he said. "Oh, this. Erm, sunbeds, that's all. I hadn't realised it was so noticeable."

"You want to cut down, mate," Dave advised, rubbing his peeling shoulder, "those things give you skin cancer."

Andy murmured agreement and bent his head over his work again. Dave noticed that Andy's bald spot was also looking pretty tanned. He wondered what kind of sunbed he'd been using.

In early August Andy came into work with a quiet little smile on his face, which for him was the equivalent of a broad grin. Dave had got soaked on the way to work again, and was in no mood to share in someone else's joy, but by lunchtime his curiosity had got the better of him.

"Alright, mate, what is it? What are you grinning about?" he asked.

Andy gave a sheepish smile.

Office Life (and Death)

"My tomatoes won first prize in the local show at the weekend," he said.

Dave couldn't think of a single thing to say about that. As far as he was concerned a garden was a place to have a barbeque and a couple of lagers in good weather, and little enough there had been of that. Another colleague who was in the canteen overheard, however, and seemed much more interested.

"Good for you, Andy! How did you manage it in this weather?"

"I have a greenhouse."

"Even so," the colleague replied, "they still need a bit of sun now and again."

"Well, the competition wasn't too stiff," Andy admitted.

"He probably talks to them," Dave scoffed, "like Prince Charles."

Andy just smiled his quiet little smile.

By the end of August, the days were noticeably shortening. Some people still talked wistfully of an Indian summer, but most had given up hope and were steeling themselves for the return of winter with hardly a breath of summer to remember. Dave found himself more and more snappish. Everyone seemed to get on his nerves. He started browsing the internet during work hours, looking for an autumn break, though he could scarcely afford it. The person who got on his nerves most of all, of course, was Andy, who continued to breeze through his boring days as if he hadn't even noticed the pouring rain and unseasonable cold. Dave stopped talking to Andy altogether, but Andy didn't seem to notice. At the end of another rainy August day, when Dave had already left, Andy picked up his waterproof jacket and set off for home, a tiny smile of anticipation on his lips.

By the time he reached his small terraced house by the railway line his trousers were soaked to the knee, as usual. The weather in his neighbourhood seemed worse than in the rest of the city, if that were possible, and in his street worst of all. Still, Andy smiled. He unlocked his front door and walked straight through the hall, out through the back door into his hedged garden. Strangely, it wasn't raining here. Andy looked up at the sky above his house, which was marred by thin cloud. He frowned, and picked up a book from the garden table. The edges of its pages were browned as if it had spent a lot of time sitting in the sun. Running his finger along the page Andy murmured some strange-sounding words. Then he picked up a handful of herbs from the table and sprinkled them around the garden. He felt his shoulders relaxing as the strong rays of the sun broke through the cloud.

Sighing contentedly, Andy sat back in a garden chair and waited for his trousers to dry, listening to the buzzing of the bees, the song of the birds, and the gentle hiss of the pouring rain on his neighbours' gardens.

Office Life (and Death)

The Job Interview

The train was late. Sullivan glared at his expensive watch again. He snorted with impatience. Ridiculous, to be taking public transport to a job interview, but one too many speed cameras had flashed his Audi, so here he was, waiting.

The nose of the train eventually slid into sight round the curved track, and Sullivan positioned himself at the edge of the crowded platform. The train hissed to a halt and the doors shushed open. Sullivan was through them before they had finished moving. Two free seats together. He marched towards them, sat down firmly on one and planted his briefcase on the other.

Settling back, Sullivan opened up the briefcase and started systematically going through the documents he had placed there the previous evening. He read over his CV on heavy white paper, his enviable references and a portfolio of recent work, as well as checking the directions to the location: Five Citipark, first floor.

The train reached another station and the passengers flowed on. People reluctantly moved bags and coats while strangers squeezed themselves primly onto the narrow seats. Sullivan's briefcase remained where it was. The train moved off, standing passengers involuntarily swaying, as Sullivan considered questions he might be asked. He heard a noise that might have been a cough. A pair of legs in pale tan stockings stood in front of him, shifting as their owner tried to keep her balance on high heels. Glancing up, Sullivan saw a woman of twenty-six or twenty-seven in high street clothes, holding a takeaway coffee. Long-ish blonde bob, all right but not a stunner. He looked back at his papers.

The cough came again. The woman was looking pointedly at his briefcase on the spare seat. Just as pointedly, Sullivan opened his portfolio wide and rearranged the papers. He was damned if he was going to cramp himself up just because this bimbo coughed at him. The tan legs remained in front of him.

Station followed station, the train jolting and shuddering, the tan legs shuffling to keep balance, until Sullivan heard someone say, "Is this Western?" His stop! Stuffing his papers hurriedly into his briefcase, he darted towards the door, which was already beginning to sound the signal for closing. He pushed past bodies and heard an angry "Hey!" from beside him. The blonde with the coffee was getting off at the same stop, but now the coffee was down her blouse. Checking quickly that none had got on his suit, Sullivan hurried towards the exit, but was sent to another queue to get a ticket. Eventually, with a ticket in his hand, Sullivan swept past the barrier. He saw the blonde ahead of him, heading for the exit. She probably had one of those monthly train passes; she looked like the type who belonged on public transport.

The rain was on when Sullivan reached the exit, and all the taxis had been snapped up by people wanting to avoid it. He saw one final taxi idling. He rushed towards it, but too late. The blonde with the coffee was much closer and was in the cab before he reached it. He was close enough to hear her state her destination, though – five, Citipark.

There were no more taxis. Hastily consulting his map, Sullivan saw that it was close enough to walk. It would probably be quicker than waiting for another taxi. Holding his briefcase over his head against the rain, he set off at a brisk pace.

He tried to concentrate on getting to Citipark as quickly and as dryly as possible, but he couldn't help thinking about the coincidence. No doubt there were lots of offices in number five, Citipark. There was no need to assume she worked for the firm he had applied to. But still the thought nagged at him – what if she did? What if she would be in the interview? Sullivan pushed the thoughts away and marched towards his destination.

The featureless white concrete and glass of Citipark looked bleak and soulless in the rain, but Sullivan didn't notice. He was nearly a quarter of an hour late. He signed in at the reception desk, brushing the rain off his briefcase, then took the lift to the first floor. Walking out into the carpeted office, he looked around despite himself for the blonde from the train. No sign of her; just a forty-something, over-made-up brunette asking him to sign in. He took a seat – nice leather armchairs, good sign – and waited, fidgeting. After a minute or two a woman's voice came through the intercom saying they were ready to see Mr Sullivan. He walked to door, took a deep breath, and opened it. A smile bloomed on his face. The woman heading the interview panel was about fifty, with grey hair and glasses. Danger passed, Sullivan marched confidently into the room with hand extended.

"Sorry to keep you waiting. You know what the traffic's like!"

The grey-haired executive saw Sullivan to the lift, smiling warmly. The interview had gone well. He was definitely one for the short-list. She made a few notes on his CV so that she wouldn't forget him in the blur of applicants, then walked through reception to her secretary's small office. It was dimmer than the reception area, so that she couldn't see the girl at her desk until she was almost at the door.

"Louise, will you see that this gets added the short-list of candidates, please?"

Louise smiled and took the sheaf of paper. The cardigan she kept in her drawer almost covered the large coffee stain on her blouse. She waited until she saw her manager re-enter the interview room before searching through the rejections pile. Selecting the CV of a Mr Sutherland, she added it to the short-list. Then, still smiling, she fed Sullivan's thick white paper into her squat grey shredder.

Floor Six

Quentin clenched his fists in concentration. Beads of sweat formed on his brow and ran down his nose. Behind the blinding light, his questioner spoke again.

"What is your name?"

"Justin," replied Quentin, squinting into the heat of the 1000-watt bulb.

"What do you do?"

"I work in a &%#ing call centre."

"Where did you get that Armani bracelet?"

"I nicked it, di'n't I?"

Abruptly the light cut out. Blinking to adjust his eyes, Quentin saw N, his superior, smiling at him.

"I think you're ready."

It had taken months of training. There was the language and accent to master, that was just part of it. There was also deportment: the slouchy walk, the slump against the wall when smoking a fag. There was social etiquette: fags should be smoked towards the edge of the no smoking zone – not too close to the doors, but not too far away, where smoking was actually permitted. Quentin remembered long hours spent learning to shoulder past people to the lift. It hadn't come naturally. Wardrobe was another consideration. For a short-term assignment, the wardrobe department would simply have provided him with suitable clothes, but that was no good for this job. He was going to be undercover for a while – a long while, if he was successful – and he would have to get a grasp of what clothing was suitable for work and for casual wear. That was a trick question, of course; as he found out after many failed assessments, work wear and leisurewear were the same.

On the morning after he was passed for the assignment, Quentin waited anxiously for the text that would come to the phone he had been issued for the purpose. He had been up since six in readiness, although he was careful to make sure he still looked as if he had just rolled out of bed.

The phone buzzed and shuffled along the table. Quentin grabbed it, opened the message, memorised the contents. Then he deleted the message, reset the phone to factory settings, wiped it for prints and slipped it into his jacket pocket. He would toss it into a public bin on his way.

The location was in the city centre, but at the shabby end, over the hill from all the elegant old buildings that lined the pricier streets. The building itself was grey and ugly, with a façade like a brow furrowed in anger. Outside, some girls smoked. These would be his new colleagues, Quentin realised. He nodded to them as he passed them, then walked through the entrance hall.

It was 9 o'clock and other workers were waiting at the twin lifts, one of which was out of order. He was careful to push past at least one person when the doors opened, but then experienced a moment of panic. He couldn't remember the etiquette for the buttons. Should he press his floor and ignore everyone else, or expect someone to press it for him, or wait until everyone else had finished and then roughly reach across them all to the buttons?

Crisis was averted by one of the smartly dressed women who followed him into the lift. Taking one brief look at him, she pressed the button for floor six. Quentin had to suppress a smile. His outfit, at least, was correct.

Arriving on floor six, Quentin half-strolled, half-swaggered into the office. The buzz of sound hit him in the face.

Everywhere people were on phones. Some played with the straws or stirrers in their drinks, some twirled on their chairs, some tried to throw balls of paper into a bin set up as a target, and some simply stared at their computer screen, but all talked. Each person had a headset on and was chattering, droning or braying away about the advantages of conservatories.

Unsure which of the small glass rooms he should enter, Quentin hovered in the corridor, hands in pockets, until someone grabbed him by the arm.

"Justin, isn't it?" said a man in his early forties. "I'm Sandy. Come into my office and I'll give you a quick induction." He led Quentin along the corridor, past more glass-fronted boxes of noise, until they reached a small office where a sulky-looking girl sat behind a desk.

"This is my secretary, er ..."

"Sarah," supplied the girl, scowling. The two men continued past her desk and through the door to Sandy's office. When he had closed the door, Sandy's whole demeanour seemed to change. There was a seriousness in his eyes, but a twinkle of mischief, too.

"Let's get the formalities out of the way. Do take a seat." He waved at the tired-looking chair. "A pity this office isn't farther up the hill; I rather like Regency architecture."

"I prefer Victorian myself," Quentin replied, completing the coded exchange that had been sent in the text that morning.

"Excellent. Welcome on board. What do you think of the front?" The man calling himself Sandy waved a hand towards the wall, from the other side of which a faint buzz of speech could be heard.

"It's very convincing."

Office Life (and Death)

"It ought to be. Most of the staff don't even know this is an anti-terrorist operation. They're selling conservatories in earnest. No, I'm not going to tell you which ones," Sandy added in response to Quentin's raised eyebrows. "It's safer that way, if anyone should be taken alive." He unlocked a drawer and took out a file marked 'Secret'.

"Now let me fill you in about your mission..."

It was top, top secret. Quentin had never worked at this level before, but never had so much been at stake either. He had done wire-tapping, of course, but never so sensitive that the activity itself had to be hidden behind the screen of a fake business. Now he found himself listening to the conversations of suspected terrorists while simultaneously reading out a script about conservatories. Sometimes he looked round at the others, wondering which ones were talking to irritated home-owners and which were trying to foil deadly plots, but usually he was too busy concentrating on disengaging his mouth from his ears.

"You need to put more into it, pal," one of his colleagues, Garry, told him during their fifteen-minute lunch break one day. "You never put any calls through to the sales team, do ya? They always give you the brush-off."

'Justin' grunted, his mouth full of sandwich.

"What you've got to do, right, is use more tone of voice and that sort of thing, enthusiasm and stuff. That way they think you're all excited about the offer. It's totally obvious from the way you read the script that your brain's somewhere else. It is commission, you know!"

Quentin nodded and told Garry he'd take his advice, but in fact if he ever put a call through to the sales team, it would not mean that someone had agreed to buy a conservatory, it would mean he had solid evidence of terrorist activity.

'Justin' made his first sale only the next day. For a few seconds his finger trembled over the transfer button. He knew he had to act fast, but he wanted to be sure. When he had no further doubt that this was a real terrorist plot he was listening to, he announced, "Thanks so much for your interest, I'm putting you through to our sales team now," and jabbed the button.

In London, screens lit up, headphones were grabbed and stenographers were summoned. In Glasgow, Garry thumped Quentin on the back.

"Well done, pal!" he mouthed.

That night being a Friday, the team went out for drinks. Quentin was in the mood for it, buoyed up by his 'sale'. He took plenty of ribbing about being so happy over one piddling sale, but he didn't mind. He took plenty of drink, too, and nearly blew his cover by inadvertently revealing that he knew the plot of one of Shakespeare's plays, but he was able to smooth it over by saying he'd seen it on TV when he was trying to impress a new girlfriend. After that he drank a bit more slowly.

Saturday passed in the painful haze of a hangover, and Sunday was uneventful. On Monday 'Justin' turned up for work just before nine, as usual, and was confused to see a large crowd of his colleagues outside the door. Some of them weren't even smoking.

"It's shut down," said one girl, who still looked hung over.

"What do you mean?"

"Cops closed us down," said another. "Said it was a scam. Wankers."

Sweat started to prickle Quentin's forehead. What on earth had happened? Despite warnings that it was pointless, he marched into the building and took the lift to the sixth floor. The glass doors were locked, and a hastily written notice on a dog-eared piece of paper read "Closed until further notice". An envelope lay outside, apparently containing some kind of legal documents that had been served.

Quentin left the envelope where it was and retreated. He walked through the cloud of smoke at the entrance in a mental fog, not even noticing. His mind chased at possibilities, trying to work it out. He was so preoccupied that he almost didn't notice the mobile phone starting to ring in the bus shelter as he walked past. The bus shelter was empty. Shaking himself back to alertness, he casually picked up the phone as he passed and answered it.

"The front was compromised. The mission continues. Go to the following address at 1600 hours tomorrow."

Quentin memorised the address, then wiped the phone, tossing it in a public bin and dropping the SIM card down a drain.

Two weeks later, a very tanned Quentin reported for work at a call centre. The location had changed, and so had the product; now they were selling solar panels. Everything else was very familiar – the smoking, the swearing, the slightly run-down nature of the building. A lot of the same team had been re-employed. Some would be government agents, the others just laid-off call centre workers happy to find another opportunity so soon. He met Garry in the rattly and slightly smelly lift.

"Where've you been? You look like you fell asleep on a sunbed."

"Tunisia, last minute thing," answered Quentin.

"Tunisia? Nice. My cousin went there last year. One of those all inclusive things, aye?"

Quentin nodded. It had been inclusive of desert reconnaissance on a dangerous terrorist cell – now smashed.

"Yeah, it was good," he summarised.

The lift opened at the seventh floor and they all traipsed out.

"Think you'll be any better at selling solar panels than you were at selling conservatories?"

"Maybe I don't want to be. Maybe I like the quiet life."

Garry chortled. "You crack me up, pal."

Quentin smiled and just stopped himself, at the last minute, from holding the door.

Office Life (and Death)

The Head of Inequalities

Richmond was Head of Inequalities at Global Resources Solutions. Nobody knew what he did. Sooner or later the question would come up, "So, what does being Head of Inequalities actually involve?" No-one had ever found out by asking. Richmond had the gift of talking in such an impenetrable and dull way that nobody, no matter how hard they tried, actually listened. But they couldn't ask him again, not when he'd kindly spent ten minutes of his time explaining it to them.

Not many people knew what Global Resources Solutions did, either. The name didn't give much away. Presumably in some way it contributed to solving problems of resourcing, perhaps with an international client-base, but then perhaps 'global' referred to the ethos of the company, or was intended to imply that it dealt with all aspects of resource solutions. Really, how could you tell? The logo didn't give anything away, either, a collection of blue stripes and shapes with 'Global Resources Solutions' written at the side. It looked just like a thousand other company logos, the name sounded just like a hundred other company names, and the premises looked like every other office in the country.

The slightly strange thing was that no-one who worked for Global Resources Solutions seemed to know what it did either. The Human Resources department hired people, organised sick cover and kept laboriously exact records, but they didn't have anything to do with the running of the company. The job descriptions they provided, and which were relayed to the relevant publications by the Communications Department, didn't give any useful clues, either: "Head of Profile Development", "Assistant to Records Clerk", "Audio-Typist", "Services Manager, London and South East".

Office Life (and Death)

The Communications Department sounded like the kind of people who might have some kind of inside knowledge, but despite all the information they passed on from one set of people to another, they only knew which publications the company routinely used for advertising and recruitment, and how to attach files to emails in such a way that no-one else in the company was ever able to open them. The adverts they placed in major newspapers, deep in the pages that nobody reads, were similarly uninformative: "Global Resources Solutions. Modern solutions to today's problems in a Global World." Fortunately nobody seemed to take any notice of them, so there were no embarrassing phone calls asking what exactly Global Resources Solutions did.

The secretaries knew all of their respective superiors' business, of course, but as their superiors always seemed to deal with very specific areas which were not directly related to the true business of the company, that didn't help. The receptionist knew everybody's job title, department, secretary's name and phone extension, and fifteen different websites which offered ways to pass the time at work. The typists knew only the names of clients to whom they typed, and the date of the last letter "of 5th of April, regarding the matter of securities". And of course, they forgot even these dry morsels as soon as the letter was sent to the post room, because no-one who writes a hundred letters a day has any desire to remember what was in them. Someone at Head Office must have known what the company did, of course, but Head Office was just a mysterious place in some little-known part of London which occasionally sent information on pay scales and growth objectives, but more often just swallowed all the records and memos sent to it without becoming any more communicative. So this was the company Richmond worked for in his capacity as Head of Inequalities.

Most of Richmond's days were spent the same way as most of his colleagues' days. He would arrive more or less on time, briefly greet the secretaries who were already there and the colleagues who were arriving, and then spend as long as possible taking his coat off, taking things out of his briefcase, turning on his computer, hanging his coat up, checking any sticky notes which had been left on his desk, adjusting his seat, putting his briefcase under his desk and rearranging the paraphernalia on top of the desk. Then it was time for the first coffee of the day. Richmond had a secretary, Joan, but she didn't see it as part of her job to make him coffee, and it takes up more time to make it oneself, anyway. By this time many of Richmond's colleagues would be making their first coffee, too, and some of the secretaries would be on their second. There was one addictive personality who would often be on her third cup of tea by this time, as witnessed by the trails of beige-brown teabag stains on the swing-bin lid. This dedicated tea-drinker arrived so early, left so late and drank so many mugs of tea (out of a large pink mug which, of course, read "You don't have to be mad to work here – but it helps!") that it was impossible to tell if the cleaners just didn't bother to wipe the stains off the bin each night or if she replenished them before anybody could appreciate their work.

    After queuing in the kitchen (a small room with a sink, mostly empty fridge, cleaner's cupboard and the coffee machine) to get his mug of black coffee, and commenting on the weather and the traffic with the colleagues trying not to touch each other in the crowded little room, Richmond would make his way back to his desk. There he would take one or two sips of the coffee, decide it was too hot, leave it to cool, decide it was too cold, and later pour it down the kitchen sink. It didn't do to drink too much of the coffee. Hot drinks at work oil the wheels of productivity, the promotional sticker on the coffee machine declared, but the drinks from this machine probably could be used to oil wheels.

Office Life (and Death)

The coffee routine was a distraction, a way of breaking up the day. There was one coffee devotee who brought in a kettle and coffee filters and a tiny carton of real milk, and the smell pervaded the open-plan office like the scent of untold luxury, but he took his filters and his kettle back to his desk after he was finished, and even took note of the level of the milk.

After making his purely decorative coffee, it was time for Richmond to check his e-mails. He clicked on the icon, and a little bubble popped up with a "bing" telling him that he had 16 e-mails. He removed the little bubble with a click and another popped up with the same "bing", telling him that he had two overdue tasks in his task list. He mercilessly burst that bubble too, and settled down to read his e-mails.

He took a small sip of coffee, grimaced, and reminded himself not to do that again. The sixteen were divided into: eight forwards of jokes, amazing true stories or amusing pictures, two of which were duplicates of each other and all but one of which he had already seen; two reminders from the Communications Department, both marked "High Urgency", one of which was about the upcoming fire drill while the other appealed to a feckless driver to move his badly parked Fiat Punto; four missives from Head Office talking about mid-term targets, but not explaining what they were; urging increased productivity in view of the sensitive state of their target market, although not specifying who that might be; seeking patience during the implementation of the new printer and fax intranet; and reminding all those who had been employed for four months or less that a decision was required of them with regard to the voluntary pensions scheme.

Richmond had been employed for six years, but still he read every word of it, including the confidentiality disclaimer at the end, which was rather overdone and seemed to imply that whatever the e-mail said, there was no reason to believe that these were the views of anyone involved with the sending of the e-mail, and that somehow you would be committing a breach of trust if you so much as read the contents of the e-mail, whether addressed to you or not.

There was also one e-mail from an online book company telling Richmond that his purchase of *Costa Rica: The Last Paradise?* had been dispatched. He already knew this because it had arrived on his doorstep that morning. Richmond deleted this e-mail, and then deleted it from "deleted items" for good measure. He knew that all other e-mails regarding this purchase had also been expunged from the computer.

The last e-mail was from Joan, Richmond's secretary, informing him that she had a dentist's appointment that afternoon and could be expected to be absent from her desk from 1pm until 4pm. Joan sat only a few yards away from Richmond, and could have told him this just by raising her voice, but for some reason she preferred to communicate by e-mail, and Richmond didn't mind. It took longer to communicate by e-mail than by speaking.

After reading his e-mails, it was time to reply to those that required replies, and forward the irritating forwards to other people who would be irritated by them. If Richmond was lucky it would by now be at least half past nine. By the time he finished replying to and forwarding e-mails and updating his anti-virus software, it would be after ten – time for his second coffee. And so Richmond's days went by, and this day was just like any other day, as far as anyone but Richmond was concerned. The Head of Inequalities, however, knew better.

Susan was the first one to notice that Richmond was missing. She was a member of the branch's finance department. She was very junior, having only joined nine months before. She was so junior she still felt slightly guilty if she checked her personal e-mails at work and she had to consult a colleague every time she wanted to forward a voicemail message, to remind her of the complicated multi-digit code required. Only the week before, she had, while making a coffee in the kitchen, asked Richmond what he did. His answer hadn't enlightened her, of course, but feeling embarrassed at not understanding his answer, Susan's thoughts still lingered on Richmond slightly and so she noticed that he wasn't at his desk when she passed it at 2.30, and wasn't at it again when she passed at 3.15, or 3.50. His computer was on, with digitally ugly flying shapes of various colours gyrating on his screensaver, but there was no briefcase and his coat seemed to be missing from the stand.

She assumed he must have had an appointment, or perhaps he had been called away. She didn't think about it any more until Joan got back from the dentist's at 4.20 ("Traffic out there, crazy!") and started asking around about where Richmond had taken himself off to. He had not left a sticky note, it seemed, or an e-mail. He had not said anything to anyone about being called away. Susan should have been working on the mid-term growth figures, but she found herself watching the slight activity around Richmond and Joan's desks, and even got up and went to the water cooler to hear better. She heard Joan saying that she would ask him on Monday; she wasn't paid to be his babysitter.

Susan went back to her desk holding the very cold water in its squashy plastic cup. She didn't know why, but she found Richmond's disappearance strange enough to stay on her mind. Maybe it was because he was always so punctual – arrived around 9, left at 5, never any deviation. Maybe it was because she didn't know what he did and, as far as she knew, neither did anyone else.

Anyway, to her surprise, when her colleagues started shutting down her computers and putting on their coats, she said she was going to work late. The explanation she gave was that if she left these figures halfway through, she would completely lose where she was up to and have to start again on Monday.

When everyone had gone, Susan, feeling like a criminal, crept over to Richmond's computer, which Joan had switched off, and switched it on again. The cleaner came in and Susan felt herself go red, but there was no way the cleaner would know this was not her computer, so she tried to look like a conscientious professional working late as the computer went through its various phases of coming to life.

Eventually the computer provided her with an entry screen – which demanded a password. Momentarily defeated, Susan started to move the mouse to turn off the computer, but then had a sudden thought. Richmond was a predictable sort of man, and not the kind to take management proclamations about the importance of security too seriously. On an impulse, Susan typed in "password" and pressed return. A message came up telling her the password was wrong. Having dared this much, Susan decided to give it one more go before giving up. The system forced you to change your password occasionally, so what about... This time, "password1" was accepted, and she found herself an interloper in Richmond's personal user area.

Sitting back in the chair with a tiny feeling of triumph, Susan asked herself "what now?" She had no idea what she was looking for, much less why. Was she going to find an e-mail about a family member who had suddenly fallen ill, and feel stupid for being so nosy? Should she just give this up now? The presence of the cleaner decided her – she would look a lot less suspicious if she appeared to be working, so she clicked on the little e-mail icon and waited to see what would come up.

There were a few new e-mails – one from Joan asking where he was, and others from the HR department and Head Office which she had already seen in her own inbox. There didn't seem to be anything enlightening in his opened e-mails either. After scrolling through them, slowly at first, then getting quicker until they were little more than a blur, Susan realised firstly that Richmond was not a man who ever cleared out his inbox, and secondly that she was getting nowhere. On impulse she took a quick look at his deleted items folder, but it was empty. As she had thought, not an inbox tidier.

Minimizing the e-mail program, Susan had a quick look at the "My Documents" folder, but she was beginning to get the picture now. There was nothing that was obviously not work-related, but then nothing was obvious at all. There were hundreds of files with abbreviated names which meant nothing to her: "pec figs 16", for instance. Almost nothing was organised into folders, and even those folders were called "New Folder" 1, 2 and 3. She opened a couple of documents at random. One was a letter to HR about his recent illness, two years ago. The next was a spreadsheet full of figures with no explanations of what they meant. Susan sighed. This was hopeless, and she should never have tried to poke around Richmond's stuff anyway. Once again she went to shut the computer down, but just at that moment there was a "bing", and a bubble popped up to tell her that she, or rather Richmond, had a new e-mail.

Not expecting much, Susan opened the e-mail. It was from an online book company. It congratulated Richmond on his latest purchase and asked him if he would be good enough to review the book company's performance in selling it to him. The book was a travel guide called *Costa Rica: The Last Paradise?* Susan thought that was rather a strange choice for Richmond – she hadn't pegged him as the exotic holidays type. But it got her no further on her search for answers. Tired now, and wanting to go home, she shut the computer down, said goodnight to the cleaner, and headed for her car.

It was in the car on the way home that it occurred to Susan that there was something strange about the last e-mail. It was strange that a man who never seemed to delete an e-mail wouldn't have other e-mails from the company, confirming his order and telling him when it had been dispatched. Why on earth would he try to hide something as innocent as a book purchase, even if it had been done on company time?

Traffic was heavy, and as she sat in the queue Susan found her mind wandering to other things she had found strange about Global Resources Solutions. For instance, she didn't know the name of anyone at Head Office, not even the CEO. She had once asked who the CEO was, but no one could remember. She was sure that she had heard that Head Office employed about twenty people, but she had never seen any of their names signed at the bottom of the frequent e-mails. She didn't even know if there were any other branch offices. And after nine months of processing the finance for Global Resources Solutions, she still wasn't sure what they actually did.

It occurred to her that she had been meaning to go to London for a while for some shopping. She could pass by the area where Head Office was located.... She told herself she was getting obsessed and should drop it. But still, why not?

Susan's shopping wasn't successful that Saturday. She couldn't find an outfit she liked. She almost decided to go straight home instead of checking out Head Office, but somehow she found herself getting off the Tube at the station she knew was nearest Global Resources Solutions headquarters. It was a dingy part of London, where everything seems dirty and no one looks like they have had enough sleep. She squeezed her handbag a bit tighter against her side as she walked.

Office Life (and Death)

    The building, when she found it, was not what she expected. It was an ugly 1960s building with a broken secure entry door. She knew that Head Office was on the third floor, and she had assumed that it owned the whole floor, but she was surprised to see a number of other businesses listed as being on the same floor, their names printed or hand-written next to the little square buttons of the intercom. Susan pressed the button for Global Resources Solutions. The button didn't look much used. The next one down, for a debt management agency, was much shinier from use. No one answered, so she walked in. The lift was broken, as they always are in this sort of building, so she pushed through the heavy door to fire stairs and counted the floors up to the third.

    The light was dim on the third floor, some of the fluorescents needing replaced. The floor consisted of a long corridor with office doors off to the left and the broken lift to the right. She walked along past dingy offices until she found one with a poster saying "Global Resources Solutions" on it, along with the meaningless corporate logo. The poster covered the whole of the glass panel so Susan couldn't see in. She knocked, but there was no answer. Inside, she could hear a very faint whirring, and the occasional "bing". She tried the door, but it was solid. Very sensible in this area, she thought; otherwise the computer doing the whirring would long since have disappeared. But what now?

    She looked more closely at the poster. It was cut to fit the glass panel, and stuck down well, but she could see that it was stuck to the outside of the glass. Taking a quick look around in case any debt-ridden clients were approaching the next office, she slowly and carefully peeled back the bottom corner of the poster. Leaning down, she looked through the gap, and saw the computer – and that was all.

There was an old-ish computer on what looked like a second-hand school table, a chair pushed carelessly against the wall, a worn moss-green carpet and leads trailing from the computer to the power socket and modem. There was nothing else. Susan wondered if she had got the wrong office, and quickly walked along the rest of the corridor checking, but all the others either had their own company names, or were clearly vacant, with empty rooms visible through the glass.

Susan went back to "Head Office" and peered through the glass. The computer still whirred but didn't seem to have any programs open. Suddenly it binged and a window popped up. Straining her eyes, her nose squashed against the glass, Susan tried to read what the message in the window said. The computer was close enough to the door and her eyesight was good. The message read "E-mail sent" and the title of the window read "Randomised E-mail Generator". Then the window disappeared. A suspicion beginning to form in her mind, Susan was pretty sure that if she waited a while another window would pop up saying just the same thing. It took forty minutes, and she was starting to feel pretty stupid, but she was right. Another "bing", another e-mail generated. Satisfied, Susan set off back to the Tube station.

Back at work on the following Monday, Susan found herself feeling less conscientious than usual. She merely played with the mid-term figures until everyone had settled at their desks and she was sure she was not being overlooked. Then she decided to continue her investigation. She didn't have access to the Communications Department's files, and she didn't think they would have any records pertaining to Head Office anyway, so she started probing in the area she did have access to – finance.

She looked at Global Resource Solutions' incomings and outgoings over the last year. She wasn't sure where the income came from, but it was clear from the outgoings that there were twenty more staff on the payroll than those who worked in this branch. These were the mysterious employees of Head Office, who, Susan now realised, couldn't possibly work there.

There didn't seem to be much else to glean from the annual figures, but Susan decided to investigate a folder in the finance section that she had always ignored. It said "Preliminary figures 2006/7". There had never been any reason for Susan, or anyone else, to want to look at out-of-date draft figures. Now it seemed to her very significant that there was a folder in full view that no one ever looked at.

Casting a quick glance around, she double-clicked on the folder. Most of her colleagues were off getting their second cup of coffee and talking about the latest reality-talent-on-ice elimination show. Inside the folder was another folder marked "New Folder". She knew she was getting closer. Clicking eagerly on the "New Folder", she was brought up short by a window asking her for a password if she wanted to proceed. She stared at it stupidly for a few seconds then, going with her hunch, she typed in "Password1". It worked. As the protected files appeared on her screen, Susan sat back in her chair and blew out her breath in amazement.

It took Susan some time to go through all of the files, picking her way around the byzantine complexity of Global Resources Solutions' central finances. She discovered that each of the members of staff who had joined Head Office had a different disability, requiring special adaptations, for which government grants were available and had, of course, been taken.

Everybody in her branch office also seemed to have some kind of special need requiring an adaptation, too, although Susan couldn't remember seeing anything being adapted. She was surprised to learn that she herself was blind, and had been provided with an outrageously expensive talking computer.

There was also a European grant for ethnic diversity that had been claimed since the twenty staff members at Head Office were of twenty different ethnic origins. A related grant had been received for teaching many of these people English. Many of the staff members were just within the threshold for top-up benefits on top of their salaries, and these were ploughed into the system. Apart from that, as far as Susan could see, the income of Global Resources Solution was derived from advertising in their spectacularly uninformative newsletter, and by the buoyancy of its own shares, the majority of which were owned by the twenty people who worked in the state-of-the-art, disability-adapted, ethnically diverse empty room in east London.

"Are you coming for lunch?"

Susan jumped. One of her colleagues was leaning over her desk, coat in hand. Susan resisted the urge to minimise the file, knowing it would make her look guilty. To anyone else, it was just a boring finance file.

"Uh, no," she replied. "I think I'll just work through lunch. These mid-term figures, you know." She waved her hand vaguely in the direction of the computer screen.

"You work too hard," said the colleague, already making her way to the door.

Susan let out her breath, which she realised she had been holding. Looking around casually, she noticed that most people were on their way to lunch. The receptionist took her lunch at a different time, but she was at the other end of the office. This was Susan's opportunity to finish the chase.

Opening up the final file, she found that it contained payment details for the staff at Head Office. They all had different accounts, but Susan wasn't put off that easily. Opening up the website for the first bank on the list, she chose personal internet banking and found that "password1" and the fictional staff member's date of birth (available in the wages files) gained her access to the account. As she expected, there were two large direct debits set up on the account. One sent all the state benefits back to Global Resources Solutions. The other sent the rest of the money to a high interest savings account in the name of one John Smith.

Carrying out the same procedure with a second account, she found the same arrangement. Finally she opened John Smith's account. Once again, the account information, this time with Richmond's date of birth and "password1", were accepted, but this time she was not ushered into the details of an account, but to a screen telling her that the account had been closed. The wages of Global Resources Solution had been paid on the Thursday, Susan knew, and the direct debits had gone out of the various accounts on the Friday morning. It seemed that the account had been closed on Friday afternoon, just before Richmond had disappeared.

Susan knew she should report all this to the police. It was fraud on a grand scale. But if she did report it, Susan would be out of a job, and so would everyone else in the office. Richmond would also be in deep trouble, if Britain had an extradition agreement with Costa Rica. Susan suspected that they didn't.

The main thing that stopped Susan reaching for the phone was the sheer audacity and flair of the thing. It seemed a shame to spoil it. So, if she wasn't going to bring the system down, there was only one thing left to do.

Working quickly before everyone came back from lunch, Susan went through twenty bank accounts and changed twenty direct debits. Later, for safety's sake, she would set about inventing a Jane Smith, open a bank account and change the direct debits again. She knew it could be done. It just took some research, a bit of planning, and a lot of daring.

Lying on a beach in Costa Rica in front of his recently purchased luxury villa, Richmond took another sip from his frozen margarita and wondered how things were going back at the office. He was pretty sure that he had covered his tracks, although "John Smith" might be in a spot of bother. He had composed an email earlier this morning on his new wireless laptop explaining to the HR department that he had been offered a job in the United Arab Emirates, which started immediately, and could he please use up his holiday entitlement instead of serving notice? He wasn't really interested in how they replied. With several years' salaries from twenty people, now wisely invested in the Bahamas, Richmond didn't think he would have to worry about holiday pay ever again.

Stretching in the warm sun that flashed and sparkled on the deep blue Pacific Ocean, he wondered briefly if anyone would work it out. But who would be interested enough in the finances of Global Resources Solutions? Resting his drink on his stomach, the Head of Inequalities drifted off to the music of gently breaking waves, and dreamt of an old computer in an empty room.

Office Life (and Death)

Company Policy on Screaming

She wants to scream. She wants to scream so often that she doesn't notice when, finally, she does. She is asked to speak to the HR Manager.

"It was just a scream. Screaming's not against company policy, is it?"

It turns out that it is.

"What about sighing?" she enquires, carefully holding it back.

About K C Murdarasi

K C Murdarasi is a Scottish author based in Glasgow. She has published short stories in a number of magazines and anthologies, from the well-known to the very obscure. She also writes novels and non-fiction. You can check out her blog at **kcmurdarasi.com**

After graduating from the University of St Andrews (the best university in the world), she spent a number of years in Albania where she picked up a handsome husband and a difficult surname. She hopes to return to live in Albania at some point.

Don't know anything about Albania? You can find out more by reading *Leda* by K C Murdarasi.

Also by this author....

LEDA

Albania, 1991: The Communist government falls and Leda, an ordinary Albanian girl, hears about Jesus Christ for the first time. Over the years that follow Albania will see many changes and Leda will have to question what she believes, and why.

When Albania plunges into the violent Chaos of 1997, Leda and her best friend Suela find themselves on the run together. Alone in the wild mountains between Albania and Greece, Leda will be forced to rely on only her faith. Will her God come through when it matters most?

Leda is available as a paperback and ebook. The paperback can be ordered from any bookshop. The ebook is available from all major ebook stores, including Amazon and iTunes.

For more information and glowing reviews, see **kcmurdarasi.com/leda**.

ISBN: 9781780881331

Acknowledgements

Thanks go to Dayspring Jubilee McLeod, my excellent copy editor, and to Cwrtnewydd Scribblers for allowing me to republish "A Recipe for Summer".

Thanks also go to all the dull office jobs I have had over the years, for providing the requisite irritation to inspire these stories, and to my former colleagues for helping me to keep my sense of humour.

Printed in Great Britain
by Amazon